T0243202

July 3, 1863—General Robert E. Lee looked over the battlefield at Gettysburg, Pennsylvania. For the past two days, his troops had taken a terrible beating here. Lee knew he was running out of time.

General Robert E. Lee

Lee was a famous commander in the Confederate army. His 65,000 soldiers were fighting for the South. Lee had won many victories since the American Civil War began in April 1861.

The Confederates were up against General George G. Meade of the Union army. Meade had 95,000 soldiers under his command.

Showdown

Lee's back was against the wall. He had lost too many soldiers already. Those left could not fight much longer. The battle would be won or lost on this hot July day.

The Strategy

Lee considered a risky strategy. What if his troops attacked the very center of the Union line? If they were successful, they would split the Union army in half. But if they failed? His men would be slaughtered.

The Question

Would Lee's strategy be remembered as brilliant or as a terrible mistake? Was the Union prepared for this attack? How would this battle impact the outcome of the Civil War and, ultimately, the future of the United States?

PREVIEW PHOTOS

PAGES 1-5: Reenactments of the Battle of Gettysburg at the actual site of the battle

Cover design: Maria Bergós, Book&Look **Interior design:** Red Herring Design/NYC **Photo Credits ©:** cover top: Bob Pool/Shutterstock; cover bottom: DenGuy/iStockphoto; 1: National Geographic Image Collection/Alamy Images; 2-3: Pete Ryan/National Geographic/AP Images; 4-5: Pete Ryan/National Geographic/AP Images; 7 top: Bob Pool/Shutterstock; 7 bottom: DenGuy/iStockphoto; 8-9: Brady-Handy Photograph Collection/Library of Congress; 10: Corbis/Getty Images; 12: David Lindroth, Inc.; 15 top: Richard T. Nowitz/Getty Images; 15 bottom: Brady National Photographic Art Gallery/Library of Congress; 16: Cameron Davidson/Getty Images; 18: Brad C. Bower/AP Images; 21: Bettmann/Getty Images; 22: Richard T. Nowitz/Getty Images; 25: David Lindroth, Inc.; 26: Brad C. Bower/AP Images; 28: Don Troiani/Bridgeman Images; 30: Alexander Gardner/Library of Congress; 32: Courtesy of Hanover Area Historical Society, Hanover, PA; 33: Library of Congress; 34: Courtesy of the Pennsylvania State Archives; 35: Jean Leon Jerome Ferris/Bridgeman Images; 36: Alexander Gardner/Library of Congress; 37: Jean Leon Jerome Ferris/Bridgeman Images; 38: Library of Congress, Manuscript Division, Abraham Lincoln Papers; 39: Richard T. Nowitz/Getty Images; 40: P. F. Cooper/George Eastman Museum/Getty Images; 41: Look and Learn/Bridgeman Images; 42 top left: Stock Montage/Getty Images; 42 top right: Don Troiani/Bridgeman Images; 42 center left: kurt/Shutterstock; 42 center right: Buyenlarge/Getty Images; 42 bottom left: Currier & Ives/Library of Congress; 42 bottom right: Strobridge & Co. Lith./Library of Congress; 42 top left: Don Troiani/Bridgeman Images; 43 top right: Library of Congress; 43 center right: Sarin Images/The Granger Collection; 43 bottom left: Don Troiani/Bridgeman Images; 44-45 background: MPI/Getty Images; 44 inset: Armed Forces Institute of Pathology/NCP 3675/National Museum of Health and Medicine; 45 inset: Troiani/Bridgeman Images.

Library of Congress Cataloging-in-Publication Data
Names: Johnson, Jennifer, 1965- author.
Title: Pickett's charge at Gettysburg : a bloody clash in the Civil War /
Jennifer Johnson.
Description: [New edition] | New York, NY : Scholastic, [2020] |
Series: Xbooks | Includes index. | Audience: Grades 4-6. | Summary:
"Explains the history of the battle at Gettysburg during the Civil
War"-- Provided by publisher.
Identifiers: LCCN 2019028956 | ISBN 9780531238189 (library binding) | ISBN
9780531243848 (paperback)
Subjects: LCSH: Gettysburg, Battle of, Gettysburg, Pa., 1863--Juvenile
literature. | Gettysburg, Battle of, Gettysburg, Pa., 1863--Personal
narratives--Juvenile literature. | Lee, Robert E. (Robert Edward),
1807-1870--Juvenile literature. | Pickett, George E. (George Edward),
1825-1875--Juvenile literature. | United States--History--Civil War,
1861-1865--Juvenile literature.
Classification: LCC E475.53 .J655 2020 | DDC 973.7/349--dc23 Classification: LCC D767.92 .D6652 2020 | DDC
940.54/26693--dc23 LC

Printed in Johor Bahru, Malaysia   108

PICKETT'S CHARGE AT GETTYSBURG

A Bloody Clash in the Civil War

JENNIFER JOHNSON

CONFEDERATE GENERAL GEORGE PICKETT led a massive attack against Union forces on the last day of the Battle of Gettysburg.

TABLE OF CONTENTS

"WHAT A CRUEL THING war is . . . to fill our hearts with hatred instead of love for our neighbors."
—General Robert E. Lee

1

A Suicidal Plan?

Confederate general Robert E. Lee risks it all at the Battle of Gettysburg.

For two terrible years, the United States had been torn apart by a brutal Civil War. It was South versus North. The Confederate Army versus the Union army.

Confederate soldiers fought for the Confederacy. That was a group of states from the South that had split from the United States to create their own nation. They wanted the right to enslave African workers.

The Union soldiers backed the U.S. government. They were against slavery and fought to make the United States whole again.

North Versus South

In 1861, the United States was divided between the Union and the Confederacy.

CANADA

DAKOTA
TERRITORY

Missouri River

MINNESOTA

Lake Superior

WISCONSIN

Lake Michigan

Lake Huron

MICHIGAN

L. Ontario

Lake Erie

VT

NEW YORK

NEBRASKA TERRITORY

IOWA

PENNSYLVANIA

NJ

ILLINOIS

INDIANA

OHIO

MD DE
Washington

COLORADO
TERRITORY

KANSAS

Mississippi River

MISSOURI

Ohio River

KENTUCKY

*WEST
VIRGINIA

Richmond
VIRGINIA

Public
Land Strip

INDIAN
TERRITORY

ARKANSAS

TENNESSEE

NORTH
CAROLINA

SOUTH
CAROLINA

MISSIS-
SIPPI

ALABAMA

GEORGIA

ATLANTIC
OCEAN

TEXAS

LOUISIANA

FLORIDA

Rio Grande

MEXICO

*Gulf of
Mexico*

KEY

- Union state
- Union border state
- Confederate state
- U.S. territory
- ✳ major battle
- ★ national capital

| 0 | 200 mi. |
| 0 | 200 km |

*West Virginia split from Virginia in 1861
and became a state in 1863.

A Nation at War

Why were the two sides fighting? The main reason was that white Southerners feared President Abraham Lincoln would outlaw slavery. They argued that without free labor, their economy would fail. At the time, there were four million people of African descent enslaved in the South.

Most of the fighting in the Civil War had taken place in the South. But in June 1863, Confederate general Robert E. Lee led his army north, into Pennsylvania. They were shadowed by Union general George G. Meade.

Gettysburg

On July 1, the two armies collided in the town of Gettysburg. After two days of heavy fighting, the Union army held the high ground. Lee was desperate.

With his commander General James Longstreet at his side, Lee rode out to survey the enemy. They gazed across the open fields at Cemetery Ridge. There, thousands of Union troops were firmly dug in.

The previous day's attacks on the edges of the Union army had failed. But Lee had a plan. He would attack the very center of the Union line. He doubted that Meade would be expecting such a bold move.

A Risky Decision

Lee announced his decision: Longstreet would lead 13,000 soldiers from three divisions on a frontal assault. Longstreet was shocked. To reach the Union line, his troops would have to cross a mile of open fields. They'd make an easy target for Union artillery on Cemetery Ridge. The plan seemed suicidal.

"General Lee," Longstreet protested, "there never was a body of [13,000] men who could make that attack successfully." Instead, Longstreet said, they should dig in and wait for Meade to attack *them*.

But Lee insisted. He believed that the Union line's weakest point was at its center. If Lee's men smashed through the center, they would split the Union army in half—and send the pieces flying. "The enemy is *there*, General Longstreet," Lee said, pointing across the fields, "and I am going to strike him."

Three Days at Gettysburg

Day 1: Confederate Victory

On the morning of July 1, 1863, a large Confederate force attacks a smaller Union force just west of Gettysburg. By 4:00 P.M., the Union line has collapsed. Union troops flee through Gettysburg to the hills south of town.

Day 2: The Union Strikes Back

By the morning of July 2, Union soldiers are dug in along the hills south of Gettysburg. Lee orders his troops to surround and destroy them. But after six hours of bloody warfare, the Union troops force Lee's soldiers to retreat.

Day 3: One Last Attack

On July 3, Confederate general Robert E. Lee orders General George Pickett to help lead a charge at the very center of the Union line.

UNION GENERAL George G. Meade, nicknamed an "old goggle-eyed snapping turtle" by his men

CONFEDERATE CANNONS blasted away at the Union line before Pickett's troops began their advance.

2

The Heavy Artillery

The Confederates launch a massive artillery attack on the Union line.

Longstreet believed that Lee was making a terrible mistake. But Longstreet had to carry out the general's orders. He found his top commanders and explained Lee's plan. He chose General George Pickett and two other officers to lead the attack.

Pickett was excited. His division of Virginia men hadn't seen any action at Gettysburg. They were eager to prove themselves.

UNION ARTILLERYMEN
fire on Confederate soldiers
during a reenactment of the
Battle of Gettysburg.

By late morning, Longstreet had all three of the divisions in formation, waiting to move out. But it would be hours before they could begin their long march across the fields. Lee had ordered the attack to begin with a massive artillery assault.

Lee hoped the artillery barrage would accomplish two things. First, he wanted to wipe out the Union cannons to keep them from firing on Pickett's men as they advanced. Second, Lee hoped to wound or kill as many Union infantrymen as possible before the Confederates attacked the Union line.

Brutal Barrage

At 1:00 P.M., 140 Confederate cannons started blasting away at the Union line. As shells ripped through the trees and exploded around them, Union artillerymen scrambled to fire back. Soon the battlefield was shaking with thunderous explosions.

One Confederate officer later described the massive barrage: "Looking up the valley towards Gettysburg, the hills on either side were capped with crowns of flame and smoke, as [hundreds of cannons] vomited their iron hail upon each other."

But unknown to Lee, his artillery assault was failing. Many shells were flying right over the Union line. Others didn't even explode. As a result, the Union lost only a few infantrymen.

Time to Advance

After an hour, the Union cannons suddenly stopped firing. Having used up most of their ammunition, the Confederates ceased firing, too. They assumed that the Union artillery had been badly damaged or had run out of ammunition. But in fact Meade had guessed that Lee was planning a direct assault on his line. The Union artillery teams were now saving their ammunition to repel that attack.

As the cannons fell silent, Pickett turned to Longstreet. Was it time to advance? Longstreet looked out at the Confederate troops. When he gave the order to march, he would be sending thousands of young men to their deaths. The general felt too upset to speak. He turned to Pickett and nodded.

Civil War Cannons

During most battles, both sides brought out the heavy artillery.

Battles often began with an artillery barrage. This was a massive bombardment intended to weaken the enemy's forces before an infantry charge began.

Long-range cannons could hit targets that were more than a mile away. They hurled solid cannonballs at buildings and large groups of soldiers. They also fired hollow shells filled with gunpowder that were timed to explode on impact.

Short-range guns fired canisters—cans packed with metal balls that sprayed deadly shrapnel in all directions. They inflicted great damage on enemy troops within 400 yards.

The cannons were operated by teams of up to eight men. And teams of four to six horses pulled the cannons into position. The enemy often targeted the horses. Without them, the cannons could not be moved.

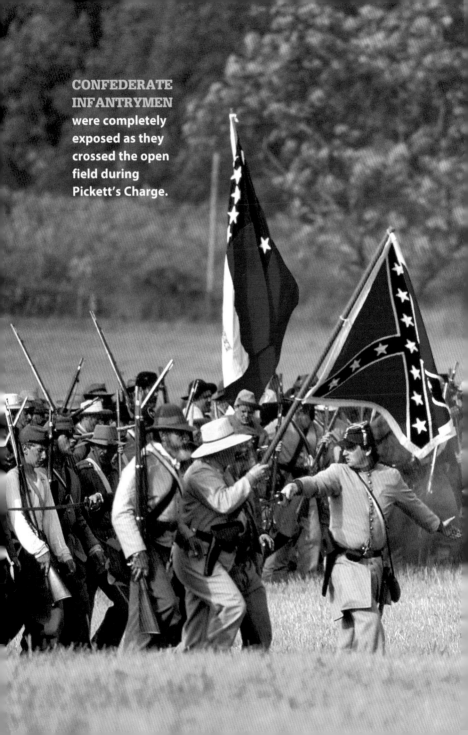

CONFEDERATE INFANTRYMEN were completely exposed as they crossed the open field during Pickett's Charge.

3

Death March

**Screams of agony fill the smoky air.
But the Confederates press forward.**

Thirteen thousand Confederate soldiers stepped out of the woods on Seminary Ridge and began to march across the fields. They were lined up in several orderly rows, one behind the next. The front row stretched almost a mile across.

On Cemetery Ridge, awed Union troops watched the Confederate soldiers approach. One Union officer said later, "[They moved] as with one soul, in perfect order . . . magnificent, grim, irresistible."

Suddenly, the Union cannons opened fire. The Confederates were stunned—they'd been certain that the Union artillery lay in ruins. But now Union shells were tearing huge holes in their ranks.

The smoke from the cannons was so thick that the Confederates could hardly see where they were going. Still, they marched on. As hundreds of soldiers in the front line fell, others moved forward to fill the gaps. Soon, some were within 400 feet of the Union line.

Now the Confederates were in range of the Union rifles. Union infantrymen behind a stone wall opened up on Pickett's men. Many bullets found their targets, and everywhere men were falling, dead or dying.

Yet the Confederates kept coming, firing as they advanced. General Pickett watched in horror as his troops were struck down by the hundreds. But he urged the survivors on.

"I never saw troops behave more magnificently than Pickett's division of Virginians did today in that grand charge upon the enemy," General Lee said later.

Pickett's Charge at Gettysburg

On July 3, 1863, Confederate general Robert E. Lee ordered
a headlong attack on the Union line at Cemetery Ridge.

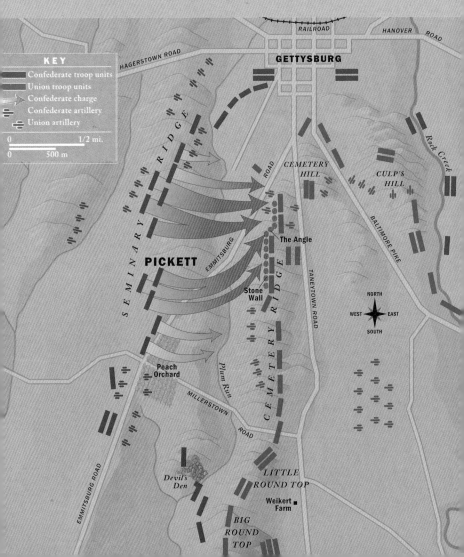

KEY

- Confederate troop units
- Union troop units
- Confederate charge
- Confederate artillery
- Union artillery

0   1/2 mi.

0   500 m

RAILROAD

HANOVER ROAD

HAGERSTOWN ROAD

GETTYSBURG

Rock Creek

SEMINARY RIDGE

CEMETERY HILL

CULP'S HILL

BALTIMORE PIKE

ROAD

EMMITSBURG

The Angle

PICKETT

Stone Wall

CEMETERY RIDGE

TANEYTOWN ROAD

NORTH
WEST · EAST
SOUTH

Peach Orchard

Plum Run

MILLERSTOWN ROAD

EMMITSBURG ROAD

Devil's Den

LITTLE ROUND TOP

Weikert Farm

BIG ROUND TOP

REENACTORS AT GETTYSBURG fire blanks at each other from close range.

4

Hand-to-Hand Combat

Union and Confederate soldiers fight to the death with bayonets and swords.

Led by General Lewis A. Armistead, about 300 Confederate soldiers from Virginia surged toward a low stone wall that shielded many Union defenders.

Facing the Virginians were Union soldiers of the 71st Pennsylvania Regiment. They were dug in behind a bend in the wall that became known as "The Angle." Nearby, a Union artillery team manned two cannons.

With his hat dangling from his sword, Armistead urged his men forward. The soldiers raced for the wall, shooting their guns and screaming. When the Pennsylvanians saw the swarms of Confederate soldiers charging toward them, they quickly retreated.

The Virginians leaped over the wall, storming through the gap in the line. Armistead ran forward to try to capture the cannons. He had just reached them when he was shot. He fell, fatally wounded.

Two Union regiments hurried to close the gap in their line. Fierce, close-up fighting broke out. Men

GENERAL LEWIS ARMISTEAD (with hat on sword) and his men charge through the Union line at The Angle.

fired into each other's faces and stabbed each other with bayonets and swords. All around, soldiers fell "legless, armless, headless," as one survivor put it. There were "ghastly heaps of dead men."

Total Defeat

Every Confederate who jumped over the wall was captured or killed. And no other Confederates reached the Union line. Pickett's Charge was over. Those who survived surrendered or fled back to the rear.

General Lee watched his troops retreat. He saw that the charge had been a terrible mistake. It was one he would regret for the rest of his life. Still, he tried to rally his men. They had to be ready for a possible counterattack by the Union army.

Lee urged Pickett to prepare his division for more fighting. Pickett could not believe his ears. "General," he replied bitterly, "I have no division now."

Some 5,600 Confederate soldiers had been killed, injured, or captured during the one-hour assault. About 2,800 of those men came from Pickett's division alone.

DEAD SOLDIERS lie on a field at Gettysburg. The three-day battle was the bloodiest of the Civil War.

"That Field of Carnage"

Lee retreats, leaving the fields of Gettysburg covered with corpses.

The battle of Gettysburg had lasted for three days. Some 23,000 Union soldiers and 28,000 Confederate soldiers had been killed, wounded, or taken prisoner.

After the disaster of Pickett's Charge, Lee was forced to order his troops to retreat. The Confederates would never cross into Union territory again. Gettysburg would go down as the bloodiest battle of the Civil War.

AFTER THE BATTLE, the July heat forced workers to quickly bury the dead in shallow mass graves. That winter, soldiers' bodies were carefully dug up and re-buried in a new cemetery (above).

The Aftermath

When the battle ended, the corpses of thousands of soldiers and horses were everywhere. Dead bodies lay in the fields and orchards, on the slopes of nearby hills, and between the trees in the woods.

Thousands of wounded soldiers had been left behind, too. The people of Gettysburg would spend many months nursing them back to health.

THESE PRISONERS were among the thousands of Confederate soldiers captured during the Battle of Gettysburg.

FORMER ENEMIES shake hands across the stone wall at Gettysburg. This reunion of Union and Confederate veterans took place 50 years after the battle.

Pickett, who had longed for glory, was left with haunting memories of the soldiers who had followed him into battle. "The moans of my wounded boys, the sight of the dead, upturned faces, flood my soul with grief," he wrote to his wife. "And here am I whom they trusted, whom they followed, leaving them on that field of carnage . . ."

Several months later, President Abraham Lincoln stood on that same "field of carnage." He had come to give a speech to dedicate a new Union cemetery at Gettysburg.

ABRAHAM LINCOLN
delivers the Gettysburg Address.

THIS RARE PHOTOGRAPH shows President Lincoln (circled) at Gettysburg just before he delivered his famous speech.

The president looked out over the battlefields. Stray canteens, cups, shoes, and horse skeletons still littered the area.

About 15,000 people had come to hear Lincoln speak. The United States was "conceived in liberty," he said, "and dedicated to the proposition that all men are created equal. Now we are engaged in a great civil war, testing whether that nation ... can long endure."

Lincoln praised the brave men who fought and died at Gettysburg. Now it was up to the living to finish "the great task remaining before us." The

United States needed "a new birth of freedom." Americans must fight to make sure "that government of the people, by the people, for the people, shall not perish from the earth."

The fighting continued for more than a year. Then on April 9, 1865, General Robert E. Lee rode to the courthouse of the small town of Appomattox, Virginia. There, he surrendered to Union general Ulysses S. Grant. After four years and 600,000 deaths, the bloody Civil War had ended. The Union had won the war and slavery had officially ended in the United States. **X**

GENERAL ULYSSES S. GRANT, on left, accepts General Robert E. Lee's surrender.

Executive Mansion,

Washington, 186 .

Four score and seven years ago our fathers brought
forth, upon this continent, a new nation, conceived
in liberty, and dedicated to the proposition that
"all men are created equal"

Now we are engaged in a great civil war, testing
whether that nation, or any nation so conceived,
and so dedicated, can long endure. We are met
on a great battle field of that war. We have
come to dedicate a portion of it, as a final rest-
ing place for those who died here, that the nation
might live. This we may, in all propriety do. But, in a
larger sense, we can not dedicate— we can not
consecrate— we can not hallow, this ground—
The brave men, living and dead, who struggled
here, have hallowed it, far above our poor power
to add or detract. The world will little note, nor long
remember what we say here; while it can never
forget what they did here.

It is rather for us, the living, to stand here,

THE GETTYSBURG ADDRESS is considered one of the
greatest speeches in American history. This is a draft of the
speech, handwritten by President Lincoln.

What Is Slavery?

Slavery is the brutal practice of one person owning another person as property.

As early as 1450, people in Africa were captured, forced onto merchant ships, and brought to America to be sold as slaves. In the 1600s, colonial planters in Jamestown, Virginia, were the first in what is today the United States to practice slavery. Slavery spread throughout the country, mainly in the South. The Civil War officially ended slavery in the United States in 1865. However, the issues and feelings raised by that shameful era are still part of our lives today.

BROKEN FAMILIES

Often, enslaved families were broken up when children or parents were sold to another owner.

ABOLITIONISTS

were the people who opposed slavery as morally wrong. They lived mainly in the North.

NO RIGHTS

Enslaved people had no rights and no control over their lives. They worked without pay and lived under horrible conditions. On plantations, enslaved workers toiled in the blazing sun 15 or more hours a day. Many workers were whipped and tortured by their cruel bosses. They had no one to turn to for help.

Timeline: The Civil War

November 6, 1860:
Abraham Lincoln is elected president. White Southerners worry that he will outlaw slavery throughout the country.

July 18, 1861:
37,000 Union soldiers march on the Confederate capital at Richmond, Virginia. Three days later, they are defeated by Confederates at Bull Run Creek.

April 6–7, 1862:
More than 100,000 soldiers fight at the Battle of Shiloh; 23,000 are wounded or killed.

April 25, 1862:
Union warships capture the port of New Orleans.

1860

1861

1862

December 20, 1860:
South Carolina secedes, or breaks away, from the Union. Other states follow.

February 1861:
Southern states form their own nation: the Confederate States of America.

September 17, 1862:
General Robert E. Lee marches north and invades Maryland. Union general George McClellan halts him at Antietam.

April 12, 1861:
War begins when Confederate cannons fire on Fort Sumter, a Union fortress in South Carolina.

September 22, 1862:
President Lincoln issues the Emancipation Proclamation, declaring all enslaved people held in Confederate territory "forever free."

December 13, 1862: Union troops are defeated by Lee at the Battle of Fredericksburg.

May 1–4, 1863: Outnumbered almost 2 to 1, Lee defeats a Union army at Chancellorsville, Virginia.

March 12, 1864: President Lincoln gives General Ulysses S. Grant command of the entire Union military. Grant sets out to destroy Lee's army.

April 3, 1865: Union troops capture Richmond.

April 9, 1865: Lee surrenders to Grant at Appomattox Court House.

1863 · 1864 · 1865

July 4, 1863: The Union celebrates its victory at Gettysburg, as well as the surrender of Vicksburg, Mississippi, after a 48-day siege.

July 1, 1863: The armies of Union general George G. Meade and Confederate general Robert E. Lee clash at Gettysburg.

April 14, 1865: President Lincoln is assassinated.

Shattered Bones

Amputation was often the only way to save a wounded soldier's life.

During the Civil War, thousands of soldiers had limbs amputated. In fact, three out of four surgeries performed in the war were amputations. Why such a high rate? Minié balls. These soft, hollow lead bullets shattered bones. Surgeons had to remove these crushed limbs before deadly infections set in.

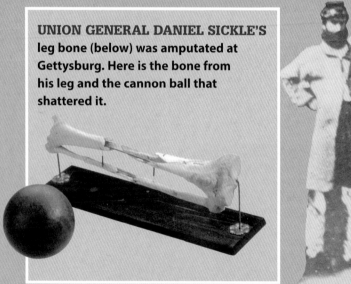

UNION GENERAL DANIEL SICKLE'S leg bone (below) was amputated at Gettysburg. Here is the bone from his leg and the cannon ball that shattered it.

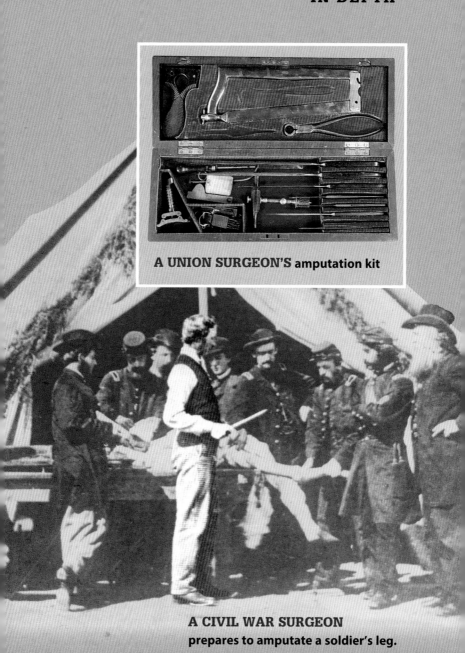

A UNION SURGEON'S amputation kit

A CIVIL WAR SURGEON
prepares to amputate a soldier's leg.

RESOURCES

Here's a selection of books for more information about Gettysburg and the Civil War.

What to Read Next

NONFICTION

Benoit, Peter. *The Civil War* (A True Book). New York: Scholastic Children's Press, 2011.

Butzer, C.M. *Gettysburg: The Graphic Novel*. New York: HarperCollins, 2008.

Fitzgerald, Stephanie. *The Split History of the Battle of Gettysburg* (A Perspectives Flip Book). Compass Point Books, 2013.

O'Connor, Jim. *What Was the Battle of Gettysburg?* New York: Penguin Workshop, 2013.

Otfinoski, Steven. *The Civil War* (A Step Into History). New York: Scholastic Children's Press, 2017.

Thompson, Ben. *Guts & Glory: The American Civil War*. New York: Little, Brown, 2015.

Wilson, Camilla J. *Civil War Spies Behind Enemy Lines*. New York: Scholastic, 2010.

FICTION

Curtis, Christoher Paul. *Elijah of Buxton*. New York: Scholastic, 2007.

London, C. Alexander. *Dog Tags #4: Divided We Fall*. New York: Scholastic, 2013.

Miller, Bobbi. *The Girls of Gettysburg*. New York: Holiday House, 2014.

Philbrick, Rodman. *The Mostly True Adventures of Homer P. Figg*. New York: Scholastic, 2011.

Ratliff, Thomas. *You Wouldn't Want to Be a Civil War Soldier!* New York: Scholastic, 2013.

Rinaldi, Ann. *Numbering All the Bones*. New York: Jump at the Sun, 2005.

Tarshis, Lauren. *I Survived the Battle of Gettysburg, 1863*. New York: Scholastic, 2013.

Westrick, Anne. *Brotherhood*. New York: Puffin Books, 2014.

artillery (ar-TIL-uh-ree) *noun* large, crew-operated guns

assassinate (uh-SASS-uh-nate) *verb* to murder a well-known person, such as a president

assault (uh-SAULT) *noun* a military attack on an enemy position

barrage (buh-RAHZH) *noun* heavy artillery fire

bayonet (BAY-uh-net) *noun* a long blade that can be fastened to the end of a rifle

bombardment (bom-BAHRD-muhnt) *noun* heavy and continuous artillery fire

border state (BOR-dur STATE) *noun* a state that practiced slavery yet remained in the Union during the Civil War

canister (KAN-iss-tur) *noun* a can packed with small iron balls; when fired from a cannon, the can explodes and the balls scatter in all directions

carnage (KAR-nij) *noun* the slaughter of a large number of people

conceive (kon-SEEV) *verb* to devise or plan

Confederacy (kuhn-FED-ur-uh-see) *noun* the 11 Southern states that seceded from the rest of the United States just before the Civil War

Confederate (kuhn-FED-ur-uht) *adjective* having to do with the Confederacy

corpse (KORPS) *noun* a dead body

Emancipation Proclamation (i-man-si-PAY-shun prok-luh-MAY-shun) *noun* the executive order issued by President Lincoln in September 1862 declaring the freedom of all slaves held in Confederate territory

division (di-VIZH-uhn) *noun* in the Civil War, a unit of 12,000 to 25,000 soldiers

formation (for-MAY-shuhn) *noun* the way in which the members of a group are arranged

infantry (IN-fuhn-tree) *noun* the part of the army that fights on foot

secede (si-SEED) *verb* to formally break away or withdraw from a group, organization, or country

shell (SHEL) *noun* a type of small bomb that is fired from a cannon

shrapnel (SHRAP-nuhl) *noun* small pieces of metal scattered by an exploding shell or bomb

smoothbore musket (SMOOTH-bor MUHS-kit) *noun* a gun with a smooth barrel rather than a barrel cut with spiraled grooves

strategy (STRAT-uh-jee) *noun* a plan for winning a battle

Union (YOON-yun) *noun* the group of states that remained loyal to the federal government of the United States during the Civil War

INDEX

Metric Conversions

Feet to meters: 1 ft is about 0.3 m
Miles to kilometers: 1 mi is about 1.6 km
Pounds to kilograms: 1 lb is about 0.45 kg
Ounces to grams: 1 oz is about 28 g